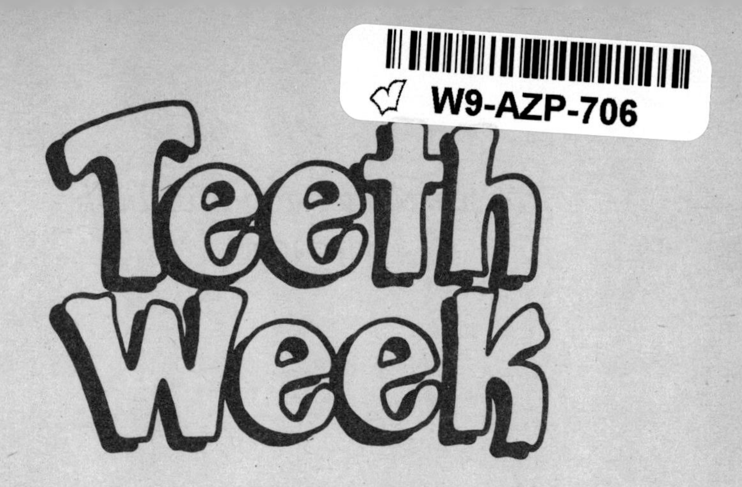

by Nancy Alberts
illustrated by Karen Jerome
cover by Fredericka Ribes

A
LITTLE **APPLE**
PAPERBACK

SCHOLASTIC INC.
New York Toronto London Auckland Sydney

To Christopher and Elizabeth,
with love

ISBN 0-590-45563-X

12 11 10 9 8 7 6 5 4 3 2 4 5 6 7 8/9

Printed in the U.S.A. 28

First Scholastic printing, May 1993

CHAPTER ONE

On Monday morning, three second graders in Mrs. Hall's room had new holes in their smiles. All three had lost teeth over the weekend.

Liza Wilson wasn't one of them. She still had every one of her baby teeth. It made her feel like a baby.

Liza was the youngest in the room. That made her feel like a baby, too. She would be the last one to turn seven. Broderick was already eight.

Mrs. Hall clapped her hands. "Three lost teeth! What a great way to start Teeth Week."

It was the first day of Teeth Week at Featherstone School. Liza hoped that Teeth Week would be lucky for her. Maybe she'd finally lose a tooth.

James, Molly, and Brian stood up front. They told how they had lost their teeth.

"I was brushing my teeth when my tooth came out," said James.

"I was out to dinner," said Molly. "My tooth got stuck on a sticky bun."

"My tooth was real loose," said Brian, "but it wouldn't come out. My dad tied one end of a string to my tooth. He tied the other end to a doorknob. Then he slammed the door. My tooth came flying out. It didn't even hurt!"

Liza shivered. She wouldn't want to do that. But maybe she should brush her teeth more often. And eat sticky buns. Maybe she'd lose a tooth that way.

James, Molly, and Brian got a big round sticker of a smiling tooth in a baby bonnet, parachuting out of a giant mouth. Almost all the kids had stickers already.

I sure wish I had one, thought Liza.

The door opened. Liza's best friend, Kelly McKay, walked in. She handed a note to Mrs. Hall and waved to Liza.

Liza was glad to see her. Kelly hadn't been on the school bus.

"Please take this note to the office, Kelly," said Mrs. Hall.

Kelly's mother poked her head in the doorway. "Excuse me, Mrs. Hall. May I see you for a moment?"

"Certainly," said Mrs. Hall. "Class, you may start on your seatwork."

Liza got out her pencil box. She took out two brand-new, polka-dotted pencils. She wished she knew what Mrs. Hall and Mrs. McKay were talking about.

"Look-ee what I did with my stickers, Liza," bragged Anna Mae, who sat behind her. "Aren't they the cutest stickers in the world?"

Liza turned around. Anna Mae had three tooth stickers. They were stuck on her folder like a triple-scoop ice-cream cone.

"Boy, are you lucky!" said Liza.

"They're stupid-looking stickers," said Broderick, who sat beside Liza.

"You don't fool me one teeny bit, Broderick Hess," said Anna Mae. "You're just jealous."

"Ha!" Broderick snickered. "They're for babies. I lost most of my baby teeth ages ago."

"I don't believe you," said Anna Mae. Neither did Liza.

"Don't believe me, then," said Broderick. He

looked at Liza. "I bet you haven't lost any baby teeth yet," he said. "You haven't, have you?"

Liza acted like she didn't hear him. She started to copy math problems from the blackboard.

Broderick chuckled. "Just as I thought. Little Liza still has all her little baby teeth."

Liza glared at Broderick.

"Hey, Liza. Don't be mad. Your baby teeth are cute." He bent down and looked in his desk. "Darn! Where's my pencil?" He reached for one of Liza's. "Let me have one."

"No! I'm tired of giving you pencils," said Liza, "and, anyway, you didn't say 'please.' "

"I just want to borrow one," said Broderick. "Please, please, please? Or I'll tease, tease, tease you all day."

"I don't care if you tease me. Just stop begging me for pencils."

Liza went to the coat rack, holding her two new pencils. She got a stubby yellow one out of her backpack.

Kelly came in and sat in her seat in the back of the room. Liza went over to her. "Hiyah, Kelly, why were you late?"

"I missed the bus," said Kelly. "My little sister fell in some mud at the bus stop. She was a mess."

"Yuck!" said Liza.

"I had to take her home to change. Mom didn't mind bringing us to school. She wanted to talk to Mrs. Hall anyway."

"What are they talking about?" asked Liza.

"It's kind of a surprise."

"Really? What about?"

Mrs. Hall walked into the room. She was holding a shiny white box.

"I'll tell you later," said Kelly.

"Okay," said Liza. She handed Kelly a polka-dotted pencil. "Here. It's for you."

"Thanks, Liza. I love it!"

Liza scooted to her seat in the front row. She dropped the stubby pencil on Broderick's desk. "Keep it," she said. "Just don't lose it."

"Thanks for nothing," he said. But he kept it.

Liza sniffed. She felt like telling him a thing or two. But what good would that do?

Besides, she was too busy wondering about Mrs. McKay's surprise. Was she planning a party for the room? Were there treats in the shiny white box that Mrs. Hall was holding?

The surprise probably had something to do with Teeth Week. She just hoped it had nothing to do with losing baby teeth.

CHAPTER TWO

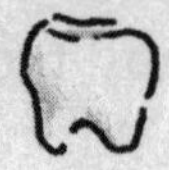

"Who remembers why we're having Teeth Week?" asked Mrs. Hall.

Liza raised her hand. So did Anna Mae. Liza could hear little puffing sounds behind her.

"Yes, Liza?"

"What's in the box?"

"You'll see," said Mrs. Hall. She set the box on her desk. "But, first, who can tell me about Teeth Week?"

Mrs. Hall called on Anna Mae. Anna Mae stood up. She went to the front of the room. It looked like she was going to give a speech.

"Featherstone School was named after a dentist named Dr. Grant Featherstone," said Anna Mae. "Dr. Featherstone was the mayor of our town for twenty years. Teeth Week is in honor of Dr. Featherstone."

"Very good," said Mrs. Hall. "Some of you may know that Kelly McKay's uncle is also a dentist. He's going to visit our class tomorrow."

Liza turned in her seat and smiled at Kelly. This must be what the surprise was about.

Liza had been to Kelly's house lots of times. There were always a bunch of freckled, red-haired relatives there. But she had never met Kelly's uncle. All she knew was that he was a dentist in a nearby town.

"Do you think Kelly's uncle has red hair like hers?" Broderick whispered to Liza. "And red nose hairs?"

Liza frowned. "What are you talking about?"

"Red hairs in his nose," he said. "When I'm getting checked by the dentist, all I can see are the hairs in his nose. Don't you?"

Liza giggled loudly. It sounded so funny. But she didn't want Broderick to think she was making fun of her best friend's uncle. "That's not a nice thing to say," she said.

Mrs. Hall tapped her foot. She looked right at Liza. "Let's listen, everyone. I have something exciting to tell you."

Liza sat up. She wanted to hear more about

the surprise. But Mrs. Hall said nothing else about Kelly's uncle or the shiny white box.

"Today, I will give each of you a poster board to take home," she said. "I would like you all to make a poster for Teeth Week. Use a slogan about keeping your teeth healthy. Like, 'Brush your teeth every day.' "

"How about 'Drink lots of milk'?" asked Liza. She wanted to show she was listening.

"Or, 'Don't have a sweet tooth,' " said James.

" 'Visit your dentist,' " Anna Mae called out.

"Good ideas!" said Mrs. Hall. "This will be a contest for the whole school. Put your name and grade on the back. The judges will look for posters that are neat and colorful and have a good message. There will be a winner for each grade."

Mrs. Hall picked up the white box. "All right. Shall I open this now or later?"

"Now!" said everyone together.

"Oh, I don't know," she teased. "Maybe I'll wait until after lunch."

"No. Now!" yelled the class.

"Very well, if you insist." She took the lid off the box.

She walked around the room so everyone

could see. Inside were different-colored little boxes that looked like tiny treasure chests. They sparkled with silver and gold glitter.

"What are they?" asked Anna Mae.

"Tooth chests," said Mrs. Hall. "Now if you lose a tooth in school, you can put it in one of these instead of in an envelope."

"Wow!" said Liza. "They're beautiful." She hoped she'd lose a tooth soon. There was only one yellow tooth chest, and she wanted it.

CHAPTER THREE

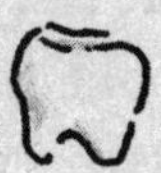

Kelly set her tray next to Liza's lunch box.

"That's neat about your uncle coming tomorrow," said Liza.

"I can't wait," said Kelly. She took a huge bite of pizza.

"Your uncle must be a very nice man," said Anna Mae, "to send in those fabulous tooth chests."

"Un-uh," said Kelly, shaking her head.

"She can't talk with her mouth full," said Liza.

"I knew that," said Anna Mae. "That pizza looks good. I would have bought some, but I have too many missing teeth."

Liza sighed. She bit into her peanut butter sandwich. She wished she had the same reason as Anna Mae for not buying pizza. Liza had simply forgotten to look at the menu.

Kelly was finished chewing. "My uncle didn't send in the tooth chests. When I was at the office, the principal told me to take the box to Mrs. Hall. All the first- and second-grade classes got them because of Teeth Week."

"Oh," said Anna Mae. She sounded disappointed. Liza was, too. She had figured she could get an extra tooth chest or two from Kelly's uncle.

"So what's the rest of the surprise?" Liza asked Kelly when they got in the ice-cream line.

Kelly looked like she was trying not to smile. "That's it. Just that my uncle's coming tomorrow."

"Oh, no, Kelly," said Liza, grinning. "I think there's more to the surprise. Is he going to bring a special treat for everyone?"

Kelly didn't answer. She was still trying to keep a straight face.

"That's okay, Kelly. You don't have to tell me. You know I love surprises."

After lunch, Anna Mae lost a tooth right in math class. Mrs. Hall gave her another tooth

sticker. Then she picked a tooth chest from the white box. At least she picked purple, not the yellow one.

Now Anna Mae had four teeth missing all together. Two on top and two on the bottom. Everyone laughed when Mrs. Hall used Anna Mae's smile as an example of a rectangle.

Liza was tired of hearing about Anna Mae. She raised her hand. She was going to show Mrs. Hall the rectangles on her belt. Her belt had pictures of flags.

But Broderick had his hand up, too.

"Yes, Broderick?" asked Mrs. Hall.

"My sister lost her four front teeth all at the same time," he said. "She was at a Halloween party. She was bobbing for apples. When she got one, a kid knocked it out of her mouth. POW! Out came her teeth. They were stuck right in the apple."

The class snickered. Liza looked over at Kelly and rolled her eyes.

"Was your sister okay?" Mrs. Hall asked.

"Sure," said Broderick. "She was happy. She was already in third grade, and those were the first teeth she lost."

Liza frowned at Broderick. She had never heard of anyone keeping all their baby teeth until third grade. He was just making it up!

"No way," said Liza.

"Bet me," said Broderick. "Just ask my sister if you don't believe me."

Liza frowned again. She began to worry. If it happened to Broderick's sister, maybe it would happen to her.

CHAPTER FOUR

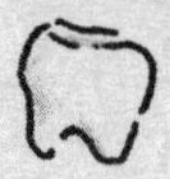

On Tuesday, Kelly could hardly sit still in her bus seat next to Liza. "I'm so excited about my uncle coming to school today," she said. "And guess what? My tooth came out in my breakfast bagel."

The tooth was in an envelope. She showed Liza.

"I have another loose tooth," said Kelly. "Look." She smiled and wiggled it. It looked as loose as a light switch.

"You lucky duck," said Liza. "I wish I'd lose one."

"You will," said Kelly.

"What color tooth chest will you pick?" asked Liza. "I hope not the yellow one."

"No, I think I'll pick pink. I hope you get one soon, too."

"Thanks," said Liza.

She poked around in her mouth. Only one of her bottom teeth was a little loose. It had been that way for a while. Maybe wiggling would help. Liza wiggled it the rest of the way to school.

At school, Mrs. Hall gave Kelly a pink tooth chest and a tooth sticker.

"My goodness!" she said. "You children are losing teeth faster than pencils."

Everyone giggled. Liza only smiled. She already felt left out. She went back to wiggling her tooth as she started her seatwork.

She wondered when Kelly's uncle was coming. She had forgotten to ask Kelly. Now she began to worry. Was he going to just talk about teeth? Or was he going to check everyone's teeth?

Talking about teeth would be boring. But checking teeth would be terrible. What if he saw all her baby teeth? He might make a big deal about it. She began to wish he weren't coming.

Liza glanced over at Broderick. She was still mad that he had teased her about her baby teeth. Then he had told that dumb story about his sister losing her first baby teeth.

Broderick was drawing pictures on the back of his papers like he always did. Most of the time, he didn't even do the work on the front.

At break time, Mrs. Hall came around to check seatwork. Broderick stuffed his papers in his desk.

"Let me see your papers," she said to Broderick.

He got them out. They looked all wrinkled.

"Broderick," said Mrs. Hall, "you've hardly started on your papers. I've told you time and time again to draw on the back only after you finish your work. Today I have lunch duty. But, tomorrow, you'll have to eat in here with me. I want you to get all this done."

Liza was nearly finished with her seatwork. She was pretty sure it was perfect.

Liza was right. When Mrs. Hall checked her work, she put a big red star at the top of each paper.

Mrs. Hall patted her hand. "Good job!" Then she whispered, "Keep your fingers out of your mouth, sweetie." She winked at Liza. "Your tooth will come out when it's ready."

Liza looked over at Broderick. He had a smirk on his face.

She tried using her tongue to wiggle her tooth. After reading class, she raised her hand. She wanted to go to the girls' room to use the mirror. She wanted to see if her tooth was as wiggly as Kelly's tooth looked.

There was a knock on the door. Liza put down her hand. Maybe it was Dr. McKay.

A goofy-looking guy walked in. He had on a gray tattered sweat suit and a blue tinsel wig. He had green makeup on his face, and his teeth and fingernails were black. He was holding a bucket. He didn't look at all like a dentist.

Liza looked at Kelly. She seemed as surprised as Liza. This couldn't be Kelly's uncle.

CHAPTER FIVE

"Hello, hello, hello," said the goofy-looking guy. His voice sounded like Dracula. "I'm Zachary Plaque. I'm the icky, sticky, yucky stuff that sticks to dirty teeth."

The kids squealed with delight. Broderick stamped his feet and whistled.

Zachary Plaque set down his bucket. He went up and down the rows, shaking hands.

"I want to be everyone's friend," he said. "But only if you never brush or floss your teeth. Only if you eat candy and cookies and cake for breakfast, lunch, and dinner. And only if you never, ever, go to the dentist!"

Mrs. Hall acted shocked. "Now just a minute, Mr. Plaque. We're going to have a dentist come visit us later today. I don't think he'd like what you're telling these children."

"What does she know?" said Zachary. He shook Brian's hand. "Will you be my friend?"

Brian giggled. "No," he said.

"You won't? Why not?"

"Because I brush my teeth and go to the dentist."

Zachary pretended to cry. "Boo-hoo-hoo!" Brian giggled harder. Zachary took a big magnifying glass out of his pocket. He used it to look at Brian's teeth. "Drat!" yelled Zachary. "Your teeth do look clean. I'll have to find someone else to be my friend."

"I'll be your friend," Broderick called out.

Liza slumped down in her seat. She covered her mouth with her hands. Zachary Plaque was funny, but she didn't want him to come near. She didn't want him looking at her full set of baby teeth. It would be bad enough when Dr. McKay came later.

Zachary walked past Broderick and Liza. He went to Molly, then Timmy and James. They all told Zachary they would not be his friend.

Zachary cried harder. "You children are not very nice. But I know how to make you be my friends."

He picked up his bucket with both hands. He acted like it was heavy. "This is extra-sweet soda pop. I want you all to have some. So when I count to three, open your mouths wide."

Zachary held up the bucket. It looked like he was going to throw soda pop on everyone.

"One, two, three!"

The children squealed and ducked behind their desks. Liza was sure she'd get wet.

The insides of the bucket came flying out. But no one got wet. There was no soda pop. Just slips of paper with words on them. They were all over the floor.

The kids bent down to pick them up. Liza saw the papers were about plaque. They showed how to brush and floss.

It looked like Zachary's clowning around was over. He began to read from the papers. The kids started to settle down. Liza gave a sigh of relief.

But Anna Mae was still laughing like a loony bird.

Zachary came over. He stood right next to Liza. "What's so funny?" he asked Anna Mae. She was laughing so hard, she couldn't talk.

Liza squirmed in her seat. She kept her hands over her mouth.

Zachary looked at Liza and winked. "And why are you hiding your smile? Don't tell me you forgot to brush your teeth before school."

"I did, too," mumbled Liza through her fingers.

"Then what are you hiding?" he teased.

"I know!" said Broderick.

Liza was sure Broderick would tell Zachary about her having all her baby teeth. She felt everyone staring at her.

She put down her hands and gave a quick smile. "I'm not hiding anything."

"Aha!" said Zachary. "Now I see why you covered your teeth."

Oh, no, Liza thought.

"You were afraid to show your teeth because they're too shiny," said Zachary. "We'd all need sunglasses."

Everyone laughed again. So did Liza. Up close, she had a good look at Zachary. She could see freckles under the pale green makeup.

Mrs. Hall looked at her watch. "Thank you for coming to see us, Mr. Plaque."

Zachary bowed. Then he took off his wig. His real hair was short, curly, and red. Red just like Kelly's.

"Boys and girls," said Mrs. Hall. "Zachary Plaque is really Kelly's uncle, Dr. McKay. He did a good job tricking us."

"Me, too," said Kelly. "I didn't tell any of the kids, not even my best friend, Liza!"

Liza turned around and smiled at Kelly. Zachary Plaque was a great surprise. And it was nice hearing Kelly tell everyone that she was her best friend.

Broderick tapped Liza on the arm. "I knew it was Dr. McKay all along."

"You did not," said Liza.

"I did too," he said. "I saw his nose hairs. They were red."

CHAPTER SIX

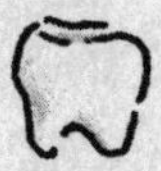

"Our posters are due tomorrow," Kelly said to Liza on the bus ride home. "Did you start on yours yet?"

"No," said Liza. "Did you?"

"No. I don't even know what I'm going to draw."

"I do," said Liza. "My slogan is going to be 'Brush your teeth a lot, if you don't want them to rot.' "

Kelly giggled.

"I'm going to draw a scary monster with brown fangs."

"That sounds good."

Liza thought so, too. She was going to make those monster teeth really ugly. She wiggled her loose tooth with her finger as she thought.

"Take your fingers out of your mouth,

sweetie," came a loud voice behind her. It was Broderick.

"Your wee little tooth will come out when you're all grown up," he said.

"Ignore him," said Kelly.

But Liza didn't want to. "I am grown up," she said to Broderick, "and I have a very loose tooth. I bet I lose it tomorrow. I'm going to take it home in the yellow tooth chest."

"Let me see," said Broderick.

Liza grinned wide and wiggled her tooth hard.

"That's not loose at all," said Broderick.

"Is too."

"Is not. I should know. I've already lost eight baby teeth. Look. My big teeth are all grown in." Broderick bared his teeth like a chimpanzee.

His front teeth did look big. Very big. Big and white like piano keys. Liza had a sudden urge to play chopsticks on them. Real hard.

"So take your fingers out of your mouth," said Broderick. "It's disgusting!"

"You can't make me. You're not my boss."

Liza stuck out her tongue. Broderick hit Liza. Liza swung back, but missed.

"Get away," said Broderick. "Don't touch me. You have slobber fingers."

"Broderick hit me!" Liza called to Mr. Jackson, the bus driver.

"She started it," yelled Broderick.

"BRODERICK!" Mr. Jackson hollered. "Get up here now!"

Liza gave Broderick a serves-you-right grin as he passed by.

"Mr. Jackson's a real pal," said Kelly.

"He sure is," agreed Liza.

"Hey, Liza, why don't you come over to my house? We can work on our posters together."

"Okay," said Liza, "if Mom lets me."

"Maybe you could even stay for dinner. My uncle will be there, too."

"Really? That would be neat. Your uncle is so funny."

The bus stopped.

"Call me," said Kelly.

"I will," said Liza. She put on her backpack and headed for the door.

Broderick had his foot way out in the aisle. Liza knew he wanted to trip her.

Liza stamped on his foot on her way past.

"Ow!" said Broderick.

"Be quiet," said Mr. Jackson as Liza stepped off the bus.

CHAPTER SEVEN

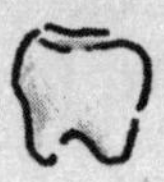

Liza tossed a big bunch of colored markers into her bike basket. Then she rolled up the poster board that Mrs. Hall had given her. She put it in a skinny plastic bag with holes for handles. She hung it over one handlebar. The bag dangled down like a punching bag.

"Remember," called Liza's mother from the window, "leave Kelly's house right after dinner."

"I know," said Liza.

"And, Liza, be careful. Especially crossing Featherstone Road."

"Yes, Mom. I know. Good-bye." Liza waved.

She kicked up the kickstand and hopped on her bike. She pedaled hard down the bumpy brick driveway.

Her bike jumped as it hit a loose brick. Three

markers flew out of her basket. Liza skidded to a stop. Two more markers popped out.

Liza looked to see if her mother was watching. She was.

"Liza! Not so fast! Please be careful."

"I know. I know." Liza picked up the markers and put them back in the basket. She turned onto the sidewalk and started off.

"Don't worry, Mom," she called back.

Her mom acted like Liza was riding to Kalamazoo. She was just going to Kelly's house. Just eight and a half blocks. No hills. No big roads, except for Featherstone, which she always crossed at a green light. No big deal.

At the fourth block, Liza turned right onto Maple Street. It was busier than Liza's street. Lots of people walked and jogged. Some had dogs on leashes.

The sidewalk was wider, but bumpier. Big roots from the huge maple trees had pushed up the sidewalk everywhere. Liza had to zigzag to miss the people, pets, and bumps. It was hard with the poster board hitting against her knee.

Up ahead, she could see a group of teenage

boys sitting by their bikes in front of the STOP, SHOP, and GO store. They were drinking cans of soda pop and laughing.

One boy looked younger. From the back, he looked like Broderick. It couldn't be. He lived pretty far from there.

Liza didn't look at the boys when she rode past. But she felt them staring at her. They made snorting noises and laughed some more.

Liza thought they were laughing at her. Maybe she looked ridiculous riding on the sidewalk, with a plastic bag thumping a beat on her knee.

At the corner, Liza stopped. She had come to Featherstone Road. The light was red.

She glanced back at the boys. She could see the younger boy's face now. It sure was Broderick. She hoped he hadn't seen her.

Liza always got off her bike and walked it across Featherstone. But this time, she wanted to act grown up. She decided to ride across.

The light turned green. Liza balanced herself on her bike and started off.

She crossed in front of a bright blue van.

"BEEP! BEEP!" came a loud honk from the van.

Liza got scared. She pressed hard on her brakes and nearly skidded into the van.

At first she thought she had crossed too soon. But then she saw that the van was filled with teenage girls. They were waving to the older boys who were with Broderick.

Most of her markers had bounced out of her basket. They were rolling all over the road.

Liza wanted to get them, but the light would change any minute. She was afraid she'd get hit. She was also afraid that the boys would really make fun of her if she started crawling all over the road.

Liza reached the other side. Her hands were shaking.

On the sidewalk, an old man pointed his cane at the street. "Missy!" he called to Liza. "You dropped something."

"It's okay," she said. "Thanks anyway."

The man smiled at her. His front teeth were missing. The ones on the sides looked like the brown fangs she was going to draw on her monster poster.

Liza shivered. She rode away as fast as she could.

CHAPTER EIGHT

At the next corner, Liza turned left onto Kelly's street. When she was two blocks from Kelly's house, she heard a bike way behind her. She looked back. A boy was riding in the street toward her. He waved to her. It was Broderick.

"Hey, Liza!" he called. "Wait up!"

Liza pedaled faster. Why should she stop? He was just going to make fun of her.

Liza could hear Broderick getting closer. The poster board sounded like a bongo drum as it beat against her knee. She kicked it out of her way. The bag caught in the front spokes, but Liza pulled it out without stopping.

The plastic handles were all stretched out. It looked like they could break any second.

Broderick was right behind her now.

"Yo, Liza," he said as he pulled up on the

sidewalk beside her. "I was calling you."

Liza was afraid she would crash into him, but she kept on going. "I'm in a hurry," she said.

"I saw you back on Featherstone Road," said Broderick. "You sure jumped when that van honked." He laughed. "You should have seen your markers rolling under the cars."

"I don't care. I have lots of markers."

At last, Liza reached Kelly's house. There were toys all over the yard.

She parked her bike in the driveway. So did Broderick.

"Good-bye, Broderick," she said loudly. She started down the driveway to the back yard.

"Wait," said Broderick. He stuck out his fists. "Which hand?"

"Forget it, Broderick. I know your tricks."

"No trick. Really. Pick a hand."

"There's nothing in either hand," said Liza.

"Is too."

"Then prove it. Open your right hand."

Broderick did. His hand was empty.

"Okay. Now open your left hand."

"Not yet," he said. He put his hands behind

his back and then stuck out his fists again. "Now pick."

"Forget it," said Liza. She turned to go.

"Look," said Broderick. He opened his right hand. A green marker cap was in his palm.

"So? What's so great about that?"

"So it's the lid to this marker." He unzipped the little bag on the back of his bike. He got out a green marker and snapped on the cap.

"Here. It's yours. So are all these." He took out a big handful of markers and gave them to Liza.

Liza stood frozen with her hands full of markers. She didn't know what to say. "Gosh, Broderick."

CHAPTER NINE

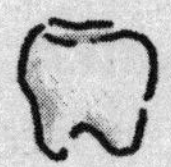

"You should have seen me," said Broderick. "I put out my arms like a policeman. Then I picked up as many markers as I could. I might have missed a couple."

"That's all right," said Liza. "At least you got most of them. Did your friends help you?"

"What friends? You mean those big guys? Nah. I know them, but I don't hang out with them."

"Who do you hang out with?" she asked.

Broderick kicked a big rock into the street. "Just some kids you don't know," he said.

"Oh," said Liza. She wondered if Broderick really had any friends.

"There you are, Liza," said Kelly as she came out the front door with her little sister, Trish. "What are you doing here, Broderick?"

"He picked up some markers I dropped on the way," said Liza.

"Really?" said Kelly. "Here, Liza, let me help you." She took the markers.

Liza smiled at Broderick. "See you later. We're going to work on our posters for Teeth Week."

"I'll stay and help," he said.

Liza and Kelly looked at each other.

"Well, we don't need any help," said Kelly.

"But thanks, anyway," added Liza.

Broderick looked mad. He did a belly flop on a pink plastic wagon. He used his hands to push himself around on the grass.

Trish ran over. "That's mine!" She tried to push him off.

"Get off, Broderick," said Kelly. "You'll break it."

Broderick stopped, but he didn't get off. He looked in the grass. "Wow! I found a four-leaf clover."

"Where?" asked Trish.

"Which hand?" said Broderick. He raised his fists to Trish.

"There's no four-leaf clover," said Kelly.

"That hand," said Trish.

"You're right," said Broderick. "Here."

Trish screamed. "Ew! He threw a worm on me! Help! Get it off!"

Liza spied the worm on Trish's pants. She brushed it off. "There. It's off now."

Trish clung to Kelly.

"That wasn't very nice, Broderick," said Kelly.

"I think you'd better go," said Liza. She went over to her bike. She took the plastic bag off the handlebar. It was stuck. She leaned down. The bag had gotten caught in the chain.

"I'll get it," said Broderick.

"No!" said Liza. "I will." She fiddled with the chain until the bag came loose.

A hole had torn in the bottom of the bag. The poster board fell out and landed on the driveway.

Broderick reached down to pick it up. Liza pushed on the middle of the poster board with her hand. "Let go, Broderick," she said.

"Gee whiz. I'm just trying to help." He let go. Liza took her hand off the poster board.

"Oh, no!" she cried.

There was a black handprint in the middle of the poster board.

"Yikes!" said Kelly. "You must have gotten

grease on your hand from the chain."

Broderick gave a loud laugh. He got on his bike. "Well, you can't blame me." He turned into the street, chuckling.

"By the way," he added, "I kept your three best markers."

Liza felt like crying. Her poster board was a mess. And Broderick had turned back to his mean old self, after acting nice for a change. She didn't really think he had kept the markers. But with Broderick, it was hard to know what to believe.

"It's all right, Liza," said Kelly. "You can use the other side." She picked it up and turned it over. But the other side was scratched and dirty from being on the driveway.

"I'd better go home," said Liza. "Maybe Mom can go buy me a new one."

"Don't go," said Kelly. "We'll think of something."

But Liza wasn't so sure. Now she didn't even feel like making a poster at all.

CHAPTER TEN

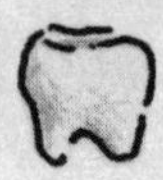

On Wednesday morning, almost everyone came to class with their Teeth Week posters. Some posters were rolled up. They had rubber bands around the middle. Others were in shopping bags, dry cleaner bags, and even giant garbage bags.

Two fifth graders came to Mrs. Hall's room. They collected all the posters before Liza had a chance to look at any.

Almost everyone had remembered to make one. Even Broderick. But that didn't surprise Liza. Broderick seemed to like to draw better than anything else.

Liza had made her poster at Kelly's house after all. She had turned the black handprint into a hat for her monster. But when she had finished making the hat, it didn't look like one for a monster. It looked more like a three-cornered hat. The kind that George Washington used to wear.

Dr. McKay had told her that George Washington never smiled much. It was because his teeth were bad. He had to have false teeth made out of wood.

So Liza had drawn George Washington's face under the black hat. Then she had made up a good slogan. She had written BE GOOD TO YOUR TEETH OR YOU'LL END UP WITH TEETH MADE OF WOOD at the top of her poster.

"On Thursday," said Mrs. Hall, "the judges will look at all the posters and vote on them. The winning posters will be the ones with the most votes."

"When will we know?" Broderick called out.

"On Friday," said Mrs. Hall.

Liza smiled to herself. A vote for her poster would be like a vote for George Washington. After all, he was voted the first President of the United States.

When the lunch bell rang, Liza grabbed her lunch and got in line by the door. So did Broderick. He pushed to the front of the line.

"Let me in," he said to James, who was first.

"No way," said James.

"You're not allowed to butt in line," said Anna Mae.

"Sit down, Broderick," said Mrs. Hall. "That is not how to get in line. Also, did you forget you're having lunch in here today? You have a lot of work to do, so start eating."

Broderick shuffled back to his seat. He dropped his lunch bag on his desk with a thud.

James led the line down the hallway. Mrs. Hall watched from the door. As they reached the lunchroom, James turned around.

"Great!" he said to the boys behind him. "We get a break from bubble-brained Broderick today."

"Yeah! Serves him right," said Brian.

The boys and girls ate at separate tables in the lunchroom. Liza was glad she didn't have to eat lunch with Broderick every day. She had seen him throw food and shoot raisins through his straw. Once he had squirted ketchup on Timmy's ice cream. The lunch ladies were always yelling at him.

In the lunchroom, some fifth graders were helping the art teacher hang the third-grade posters on the walls.

The second-grade posters were already up. Liza spotted hers right away. George Washington's black hat was as big as a bat's wing. But the words of her slogan looked small. She should have made them bigger.

Liza looked at Kelly's poster. It was so neat-looking. It had a picture of a red-haired dentist in a white jacket. The slogan said DENTISTS ARE GREAT!

Liza looked at the others. None of the posters had names on the front because of the judging. One looked like a blue-and-green jellyfish. It was supposed to be Zachary Plaque. BOO TO ZACHARY PLAQUE, it said.

There was one poster that everyone seemed to be looking at. It had a simple slogan—MAKE FRIENDS WITH YOUR TOOTHBRUSH. The letters were big and bright.

It had a drawing of a giant toothbrush shaking

Boo
to Zachery
Plague

hands with a boy. The toothbrush looked like a person. The brush part was the face. The handle was the legs. The hands were coming out of the handle.

Liza kept looking at it while she ate her lunch. She had to admit it was one of the best second-grade posters. Maybe the best of all. She hoped it was a third-grade poster that had gotten mixed up with the second-grade ones.

CHAPTER ELEVEN

The lunch ladies called the first tables for recess. When Mrs. Hall's tables were called, everyone rushed over to the big cans to dump trash. Liza dropped a Dixie cup lid on the floor. Before she could get it, Timmy slipped on it and fell down. He bumped his face on the trash can rim.

Timmy started to cry. Liza bent down to see if he was all right. But a lunch lady shooed her outside.

"Next time, be more careful," she scolded Liza.

Liza worried all recess. But when the bell rang, Timmy was back in class, all smiles. He had knocked out his very first baby tooth. Now he had a tooth sticker and a red tooth chest to show for it.

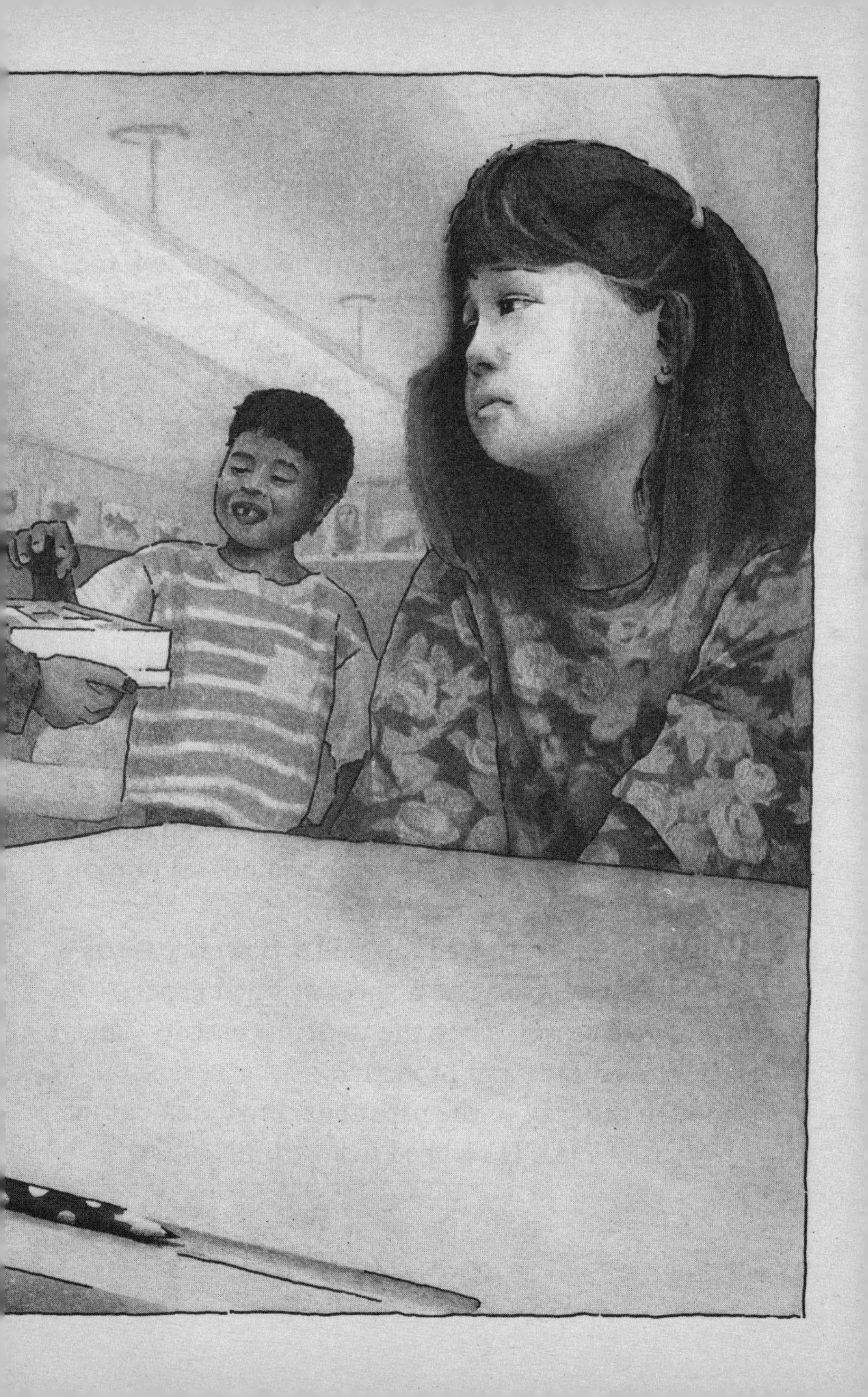

Liza felt terrible. She put her head down on her desk.

"I think you children are overworking the Tooth Fairy," said Mrs. Hall. "She needs a vacation."

Everyone giggled. Everyone but Liza. Now she was the only one in the whole class with all her baby teeth. Did Broderick really have a sister who didn't lose one tooth until third grade?

"How's your little tooth today?" Broderick whispered to Liza while Mrs. Hall wrote on the blackboard.

Liza kept her eyes on the blackboard as she wiggled her tooth with her tongue.

"I bet you're glad Timmy didn't pick the yellow tooth chest," said Broderick.

Liza felt her face getting hot. Of course she was glad. But she wished she had not told Broderick that she wanted the yellow one.

Mrs. Hall turned around. "Paper passers, please give everyone a sheet of lined paper."

Paper passers sat in the front row of seats. That included Liza and Broderick.

On the way to the paper box, Broderick cut in front of Liza. He jabbed her with his elbow.

"Ow!" yelled Liza. "That hurt!"

Mrs. Hall went over to Liza and put her arm around her. "Broderick," she said sternly, "please act like a gentleman. Now, what should you say to Liza?"

"I'm sorry," he said in a not-very-sorry-sounding voice.

"Thank you, Broderick," said Mrs. Hall. "I think you're just eager to start on your spelling."

Broderick smiled his piano key smile. Liza sighed as she wrote her name between the lines. Mrs. Hall could be strict. But she never lost her temper. She was nice to everyone. Even Broderick.

Broderick picked a fight with a fourth grader on the bus ride home. He had to sit by Mr. Jackson again.

"Look who's in trouble again," Liza said to Kelly.

"My uncle said he probably acts the way he does because he wants attention," said Kelly. "I wonder if he feels bad about being in second grade again."

Liza wondered, too. She had never thought about it before. He was the only repeater in the room. She felt bad enough being the youngest in the room and the only one with all her baby teeth.

Maybe Broderick felt bad, too. Maybe she should try being nice to him. Mrs. Hall was always saying, "To make a friend, you have to be one."

When it was time for her to get off the bus, she turned to Broderick on her way past his seat.

"Good-bye, Broderick," she said with a smile. "I'll see you tomorrow."

Broderick said nothing. He didn't even smile back. He stuck out his tongue.

Liza turned away, upset. Well, she thought, I tried.

CHAPTER TWELVE

Mrs. Hall was not at her desk the next morning. A tall, skinny lady with frizzy hair stood in front. She didn't look much older than Liza's teenage baby-sitter.

"Good morning, boys and girls. My name is Miss Twitchell," she said in a squeaky voice.

Liza thought she looked scared. Maybe this was the first time she had ever been a substitute. Liza hoped not. Some of the kids gave the last substitute a hard time.

"Good morning, Miss Twitch-ee," said Broderick.

It didn't feel like a good morning to Liza. Not good at all. It wasn't even nine o'clock and already the kids were restless.

"Oh teacher, oh teacher," Broderick called out.

"Yes?" said Miss Twitchell.

"I lost my tooth on the bus this morning. See?"

Liza spun around in her seat to look. Broderick was holding up a small, white object. It did look like a tooth. A real baby tooth.

"That's just the tooth you carry around for good luck," James called out.

"No, it isn't." Broderick turned around and gave James a dirty look. "I lost it this morning."

"That's great," said Miss Twitchell. "You can put it under your pillow tonight."

"Yes, Miss Twitch-ee. I mean, Miss Twitchell," said Broderick. "Mrs. Hall always lets us have a sticker and a tooth chest to put it in."

He got up and walked to Mrs. Hall's desk. "She keeps them in there." He pointed to the white box.

"Well," said Miss Twitchell. "Mrs. Hall will be back tomorrow. Why don't you ask her then."

Some of the kids went along with Broderick. It was like they were trying to get him in trouble.

"She always lets us," said Molly.

"Sure," said Brian. "Even when she's not here."

The kids were having fun. Liza didn't think it was fun at all. She wanted to holler, "No fair! No fair!" But no one would listen. Not even Miss Twitchell.

"Well, then, I guess you can have one."

Liza held her breath as Miss Twitchell opened the white box. She handed Broderick a tooth sticker and a blue tooth chest.

Liza let out her breath. At least he didn't get the yellow one.

"No," said Broderick. "We get to choose."

Liza held her breath again. Maybe he wouldn't choose the yellow one. Especially since she had tried to be nice to him on the bus.

"Let me see," said Broderick, taking his good old time. Then he looked right at Liza. "I'll take this one." He held it up for all to see. It was yellow.

Liza shut her eyes and tried not to cry. Kelly patted her on the back as she went past to sharpen her pencil.

"Now, boys and girls," said Miss Twitchell. "It's time to start our work. Open your spelling books to page thirty-eight."

The morning dragged on. Broderick did not

behave. He acted like he didn't know how to spell his name. He hummed during silent reading time. He sent three paper airplanes out the window.

After lunch, Broderick acted wilder. The class got louder. Broderick drew a frizzy-haired, frowny picture of Miss Twitchell on the blackboard. Miss Twitchell got upset. By the end of the day, she had turned downright mean and grouchy.

It was the worst day in Liza's entire life, and it was all Broderick's fault.

Miss Twitchell just didn't know what to do with Broderick. Mrs. Hall would have known.

If Liza were the teacher, she would have marched him down to the office first thing in the morning. Before he even got near that yellow tooth chest. That would have wiped off his piano key smile.

CHAPTER THIRTEEN

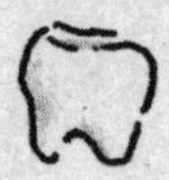

Finally school was over. Liza stood sullenly in the bus line. It had been a terrible day. A terrible week. Teeth Week had not been lucky for Liza at all. Only one day left and she still had all her baby teeth.

Kelly joined Liza in line. "Cheer up," she said. "Mrs. Hall will be back tomorrow. Miss Twitchell said so."

"That Miss Twitchell makes me so mad," said Liza, "but not as mad as Broderick does."

Broderick was already on the bus in his new seat up front. Liza could see him through the window. He was punching the air like he did on the playground to scare kids. Mr. Jackson was standing outside, talking to one of the teachers.

Kelly got on the bus. Then Liza. Broderick was still punching the air. All of a sudden, Liza's lunchbox sprang open. A half-eaten peanut butter sandwich plopped on the floor. But as she stooped to pick it up, Broderick's fist landed smack on her mouth.

"Oo—OWW!" Liza wailed, with her hand at her mouth.

"Oops!" said Broderick. "I didn't mean to."

"Now what?" said Mr. Jackson as he ran up the steps of the bus.

"I really didn't mean to this time," said Broderick. "She put her mouth where my fist was."

"Now I've heard everything," said Mr. Jackson. He turned to Liza. "Are you all right?"

Liza glared at Broderick. "No," she said, as she sat down. Then she saw blood on her hand. "I'm bleeding!" Kelly gave her some tissues. Liza held one over her mouth. "I think he cut my lip."

"Ew!" some kids moaned when they saw the blood.

Broderick looked pale. "Gee Liza," he said. "I'm sorry. I really am!"

Mr. Jackson shook his finger at Broderick. "You'd better be sorry."

Suddenly Liza stopped crying. "Wait a min-

ute," she said. She felt an empty spot in her bottom row of teeth. "My tooth! It's gone! I lost my first tooth!"

Liza looked in the tissue. "But where is it?" She looked on the floor. So did Kelly.

"I'm sorry, girls," said Mr. Jackson. "You'll have to sit down. I've got to get this bus rolling. If I find your tooth, I'll save it for you, Liza."

The girls sat down.

"You might have swallowed it," said a fifth-grade girl in the seat across from them.

"Oh, no!" Liza felt her throat. She tried to imagine her tooth going down.

"It won't hurt you," said Kelly. "My brother swallowed a tooth once."

"I wanted to take it to school tomorrow," said Liza, "and pick out a tooth chest for it. But now that the yellow one's gone, I guess it doesn't matter."

She glared at Broderick six rows up. He couldn't have been sorry. He was acting up again. She could see him crawling on the floor. He was probably up to one of his tricks again. Like unraveling someone's sock. Or sticking gum on someone's backpack zipper.

"I'm sure Mrs. Hall will let you pick a tooth chest anyway," said Kelly. "There are lots of pretty ones left."

"I know," said Liza, "but I really, really wanted the yellow one."

Finally she had lost a tooth. But she hadn't counted on losing it altogether.

CHAPTER FOURTEEN

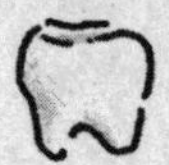

Standing at the bus stop on Friday morning, Liza felt better. When she woke up, she had found a dollar under her pillow. The Tooth Fairy had come even though Liza had no tooth to leave her.

She also had noticed that a tooth next to the new space felt loose now.

The bus came. Liza got on. She walked by Broderick without looking at him.

A big box of cupcakes, covered with clear plastic, was on Kelly's lap.

"Yum. They look good!" said Liza.

"It's Trish's birthday," said Kelly. "I'm going to carry them into her kindergarten class."

"Happy birthday!" Liza said to a smiling Trish one row back.

She showed Kelly her loose tooth.

"Terrific," said Kelly.

"And the Tooth Fairy left me a dollar last night," said Liza.

"Double terrific!" said Kelly.

"Triple terrific is Mrs. Hall being back at school today," said Liza. "I'm going to ask her to make Broderick give back the yellow tooth chest."

"Do you think he will? What if he lost it or broke it?"

Liza hadn't thought about that. She sat quietly the rest of the way to school.

At school, they got off the bus. Kelly took Trish's cupcakes inside. Everyone else stood in groups on the playground, waiting for the bell to ring.

Liza stood by herself. She didn't feel like talking to anyone.

Broderick walked over. He held out his fists. "Which hand?" he asked.

"Get away!" He was the last person she wanted to see.

"Pick a hand," he said, smiling.

Liza turned around. Did he think she was going to fall for that trick again? It was probably

another worm, or something worse, like a dead cricket.

"Here." Broderick dropped something into her back pocket.

Liza screamed. She pulled whatever it was out of her pocket and flicked it on the ground.

It was not a worm or a dead cricket. It was a small white package. She picked it up carefully. It rattled.

Under layers of tape and toilet paper, Liza found the yellow tooth chest. Inside was a tooth.

"You can have the tooth chest," said Broderick.

Liza smiled. "Thanks, but I don't want your tooth."

"It's yours," he said. "I found it on the bus after you got off yesterday."

"Gosh, Broderick," said Liza as she held the tooth chest tightly. "Thanks!"

CHAPTER FIFTEEN

The bell rang. Liza marched into class, teeth first. Mrs. Hall saw the space right away.

"Oh, my goodness, look! Liza has joined the ranks of the toothless."

Everyone clapped. Even Broderick. Everyone seemed happy for Liza.

"How did it come out?" asked Mrs. Hall.

Liza smiled at Broderick. "Someone bumped me," she said. "It was just an accident." She stood tall as she waited for her tooth sticker.

The loudspeaker crackled. "May I have your attention?" came the principal's voice. "I have the names of the winners of the Teeth Week Poster Contest."

The poster contest. Liza had forgotten all about it. There was a buzz of excitement in the room. Liza went to her seat and sat up straight.

"Please send the winners to the office after I call the names," said the principal. "There is a plaque for each winner."

Plaque? What kind of prize was that? Liza wondered.

The kindergarten and first-grade winners were called. Second grade was next. Liza crossed her fingers.

"The winning poster of second grade is 'Make friends with your toothbrush,' by Broderick Hess."

There were gasps and groans and a few "boo's." Liza was shocked. Broderick's poster was the one that everyone had been looking at.

Mrs. Hall frowned at the boo-makers. She went over and hugged Broderick. "Wonderful," she said. "I'm so proud of you."

Broderick looked embarrassed. His ears were red. He left for the office.

Liza felt terrible. Broderick did have the best poster. But no one seemed happy for him. He was like Zachary Plaque. He had no friends. It was as if his toothbrush, like the one on his poster, was his only pal.

It was his own fault. He was a real trouble-

maker and he acted mean. But he also could be funny, and sometimes even nice.

Liza suddenly decided something.

She might be the last one to turn seven and the last one to lose her first baby tooth. But she would be the first one to congratulate Broderick.

When he walked back into Mrs. Hall's room, she stood up. "Congratulations!" she said. "Three cheers for Broderick."

Mrs. Hall gave her a pleased smile. She helped Liza lead the cheer.

"Hip, hip, hooray! Hip, hip, hooray!" they said.

"Come on, everyone," said Liza. Kelly stood up and joined the cheer. Soon everyone was standing.

"HIP, HIP, HOORAY!" they all said together.

Broderick's ears got redder than ever. He grinned at Liza and the rest of the kids.

He held up his plaque. It was made of wood and metal, not the icky, sticky, yucky stuff on teeth. It had Broderick's name on it.

Broderick let Liza hold it first. She smiled, showing the space in her mouth.

Teeth Week had turned out all right after all.

ABOUT THE AUTHOR

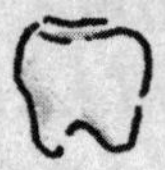

Nancy Markham Alberts relives her own childhood through her writing. Her years as an elementary schoolteacher and the antics of her school-age children and their friends provide additional inspiration.

She grew up in southern New Jersey, but now lives near Pittsburgh, Pennsylvania, with her husband and their two children.